THE PROPERTY OF

Castle Haystack

A Study by
Oscar Writenhous
of
the Journal Parchments
of Professor Eff Ceffsky

William W. Steidel

Author and Illustrator

Cover art and story artwork by William W. Steidel.

Edited by Caitlyn M. Schmidt and S. C. Moore.

ISBN: 978-1-938281-77-8 (hardcover)
ISBN: 978-1-938281-78-5 (paperback)
ISBN: 978-1-938281-79-2   (e-book)

Library of Congress Control Number: 2019915650
Published 2019, Castle Garden Publications,
an imprint of Gazebo Gardens Publishing, LLC.

www.GazeboGardensPublishing.com

Printed in the United States of America.

I, Oscar Writenhous, am the one responsible for the study of the pages found here within. I was overwhelmed with emotion when a friend carefully lay into my hands the parchment journal pages ravaged by time, worn, and delicate. That was my introduction to the journals of Professor Eff Ceffsky, who was shipwrecked on a beach centuries ago.

The professor's journal parchments represented within this book have three distinct characteristics—his notes, drawings, and personal observations. His explanations and emotions drift about like illusive shadows and are so entwined with facts, they become bewildering.

Three people were involved in the production and publication of this work. First and foremost is the architect of the original journal, Professor Eff Ceffsky. Second is William W. Steidel, the illustrator of the additional pages and images within the journal. Third is myself, the historian who conducted the study.

The original parchment pages were reproduced as found, however fragmented they may be. The condition of these parchments, the amount of destruction and decay, the many bits and pieces, and their fragility, created a problem similar to that of a jigsaw puzzle. I have attempted to clarify this in my study.

Any vacancies that occur are a void caused by a parchment from the journals long vanished or too damaged to be used. I made no alterations to the pages—no edits were done to the text for spelling or mechanics. My personal comments are printed in italics where I saw a need to add explanation.

Problems did occur. The exact intent of the professor's notes within his journals was, at times, in question. Various solutions were reached with research and counsel from my colleagues.

I made only one request of the illustrator, that he adapt his technique to best match the original works of the professor. I was not far into this study when I realized that by using Mr. Steidel's abilities, we could solve other problems. There were times when the text itself described a visual concept that cried out to be illustrated: the areas within the castle that the professor referred to as Harbor Hall, on a two-page spread, and the Great Hall, also on a two-page spread. They should not be mistaken for Professor Ceffsky's original sketches. The division between the original sketches and those of Mr. Steidel need no clarification. Although nearly identical in style, the difference is discernible.

I have, I believe, the most complete collection of facts and information pertaining to the subject presented in this manuscript. My intent is to present the data in such a way that the incompleteness of these journal entries and drawings have continuity. Now, with what was recovered of the journals of Professor Eff Ceffsky, there is validity to what has long been rumored.

Four centuries ago on the North Pacific Coast,
not far from Ecola Creek, there was a shipwreck.

All aboard were lost to the sea.

All but one.

His journals were found.

The village is quiet. Most have sought shelter, the day being rain. I sit before a fire. I feel well enough this day to continue my journals. How long I lay unwell I know not, nor is it known to me the time, the day or month. I know the month being July or August. I am confused of mind. I believe August. I can not be precise. So I designate this day day One of my travels in this strange, beautiful land. I am in lingering pain. My left arm wrapped in moss and straw is held tight to my chest like a cocoon with twine and cloth, a rough fiber.——— I try to remember....

    Beyond the fire they squat before me... smiling.....watching me... I feel faint...

    They are gone,... they were here a moment ago.....now they are gone...I hear the wind... the rain. The fire is poked, sparks rise into the darkness....This I remember!...the wind... the sea.....I am in my bunk....the bell....the ship's bell, ringing urgently, frantically,...danger...I remember the storm. A horrendous storm! the ship rolls sharply. I am thrown from my bunk,..my body whipped against something sharp! pain!! Darkness all round.... Someone screams...I... gasping for air,... a gurgling noise....someone drowning! a horrid sound. the ship rolls uncontrollably.. Again I am thrown across the cabin.—— Water rushes in... debris all about.. I hear wood splintering, water floods over us.... the ladder!...a way to escape. the ship being thrown about as if in the——

grip of some huge beast.....We are an intrusion.
we are nothing. Again forced across the cabin
floor.   entangled, wedged into
the passageway,...so cold.....the ladder!...I
feel the rail,...I pull myself up. the bell
ringing....I cannot move,   wedged
against   I push my
hand against   to free myself.
...I
      open!......I   fling myself
      against the hatch.   It gives. I see the mast
high above. A thin slice of moon swings about
it drunkenly. Sails, lines, block and tackle
   thrash around it like some monster with
many tentacles.
           the bell ringing more frantically now....
some poor soul frozen in terror to his chore.
It is a ship no longer alive, a carcass now
broken and dying.... With constant...
   deliberateness the raging sea reeks its
havoc....the ship's bell rings unsteadily, chaotically
uncontrolled, then nothing,
gone, washed away, taken by the sea.. High
above I hear a crack.....I remember.
I looked up to see the mast with canvas, and all
its rigging plummeting toward me, crashing upon
me. My arm caves in.... Pain!....Clawing, I try
to free myself...entwined in lines and debris...
I cannot! Water rushes over me, cold wet
darkness. I surrender.   with abandon I
give myself to the sea.

            I was hers.

I struggled for consciousness only to find myself in
an unearthly atmosphere—the air was moist and hot, too
hot to breathe. My eyes refused to focus. Was I blind? All
was a fog, and that fog was unbearable . . . I tried to raise
my body, but I could not. A great weight was upon my chest
forcing me down. I tried to scream, but my cry was
stifled as hot air scorched my lungs. Sweat flowed
from every pore of my body. Was this the end of life? Did
I drown? Am I now being roasted alive—was this to be
my fate? Blurred images floated in my head; reality
evaded me, I heard voices, a draft of cool air, a loud
hissing sound, a face appeared before me. A soft,
round, brown face with eyes of light tan, pupils
black, stared at me, then a smile, broad and warm. He
spoke. I did not know the language, but I understood.
I had wakened in a small native steam hut. By my
side and caring for me was a native man
who was to become my good friend. His
name is Hipko. He laid his hand on

my chest to comfort me, and let me
know I was safe. Another squat figure came in
through a small opening bringing with him

a cool breeze. On a board he carried a red hot rock. He put this on the ground with other rocks and left. Hipko then took a wooden scoop from a wooden trough and poured water upon the rocks. Steam hissed and immediately filled the small chamber.

Day 1... only now many days later, have I learned of my rescue. Hipko had found me floating in the surf on a cargo hatch. At first I was assumed dead, for there were others, and they were. I was the only survivor. I lay delirious for days and the steam baths given me were the natives contribution to my recovery. And I have since learned that most illnesses inflicted upon the inhabitants of this villiage receive the same treatment. I have also found that frequent trips to that little hut not unpleasant.

I have been eating well. Strength once again enters my body. Day 19 — Some remains of the ship and its cargo have been found. Each day some small article or piece of clothing is found, and there is a great deal of excitement and wonder among the natives. I find myself not in a position to lay claim to any of these items, nor do I feel I should. Many of the villagers wear these articles as adornments. This action does cause me some sadness. There is only one item for which I show any affection, my own small sea chest, its contents were damp but undamaged. I let it be known that this was my property, and with Hipko's insistence it was returned to me.

— The village is busy making a large canoe. Its length does amaze me. When finished it will carry some thirty people and all their goods. Progress has been so excellent that they expect it to be in the water by next full moon. A large tree of specific size and kind is found. Then with the crudest of tools; stone axes, spear points, shells and bone they chop and scrape to fashion the shape. Everyone in the village seems to have a job to perform the length is marked off. I myself found it to be 17 paces long. Its center is hollowed out. For this the tool most commonly used is fire. The black burnt wood is easily chipped away until new wood is exposed and then the process is repeated. I watched and marveled at their ability to fashion such a beautiful object in so short a time. Crossbars are placed from side to side just below the gunnal. They themselves are tapered out so as to deflect the water. Those sections that are close to completion are scraped smooth with bone or shell. The work would be the envy of any shipbuilder. The final process is to carve and paint various sections, making what is fine even finer. The bow peice is given the greatest attention; this being comprised of many sections fitting together in the most intricate manner using no nails or pins. Day 22— A short distance south on the beach is a strange old stump of a tree and it is of great importance to the villagers.

they stand in a line going no further than this. I did not have been curious alwa
sane
es interest me
large outcrop
the scale i
of s n indiscernible. It does erest it
is y intention to explore. The local
Those whom I thank for my rescue dare not to go
near this monolith they have many odd customs
id fear the object. When the wind is about, a sound is
heard from this shadowy formation - a moaning and
howling which is indeed frightful. the natives beleive it
haunted; inhabit some leg of the Past so afraid
they dare not go near it. And invisible barrier
stretching from shore trees down across the sand
to the water's edge. A line they dare not cross a prominent
monument declaring this boundary. If they wish to go
south, they travel a path around this monument into
the forest. A grotesque tree stump decorated with

nd there are ma   species
uch birds th   argest being
head of white and   wingsp
t does tish fo   sal   on is very
i find to be the smallest
nd seems never
fear the bea
stop. T
Hipke

zenth
with its
a bill as La
eating. —Da
only a shor
puzzles me s
Large marker
superstit   Wh   ar
gressive
AND PO   in

wonder coul   it be. I was   a
goal dark   nst the   orning T
sky. After a few steps I turned to look
back. They h   not moved.
standing   a line
that did n   exist
Some beckoned me to return
a   y, others stood   with hands over their   ouths
I   waved to assure t   a, all was well b   as I
a   in turned to face my objective, that huge
mo   olith was gone. A fog ha   come in and had
engulfed it. and I t   was so   to be its victim.
Whe   look   o back at my   friends. I
felt the cool mist about me. then I knew that
I also had disappeared from their view. then a
eerie moaning was heard, and alone with only
the sound of the surf to guide   me
A chill was apon m   it   as not   the fog. That

Day 43 ... the pillar I found is indeed an object made by man ... but who? the workmanship is excellent, but, I feel beyond the capabilities of the local natives. The stones are well shaped and the mortar does glisten when the sun shines upon it.

West

Found a favorable campsite protected from the wind by large trees and warmed by the afternoon sun.

I devised my own means of measure. I cut a stick to my exact height, then by spreading my hands, end over end, I find it to be eight and one half hands long. I can therefore at any future date, convert to known measures.

thirty paces west of here I find the fondation of a similar relic. Mortar rock and size being almost identical.

From here I see ... the monolith to be a phenomenon of nature ... the tide is high and forbids closer examiation ...

3½

2½

three small objects found on my walk

and in my campsite have begun building a shelter. A few natives hide in the forest. Watching my progress and do not venture forth. They have a fear of this area, a mystery I have yet to solve....

Did find an object of interest buried in the sand; some fragment of a wrecked ship, perhaps mine.

Day 49~
The weather misty yet mild. My friend Hipko and three natives appeared from the forest. They are assisting in building my shelter. Their knowledge and help I receive with great joy.

The process of splitting the timbers and producing planks with such crude tools is a wonder to watch. The wood used is the same as that used in the construction of their lodges... It is most aromatic.

Location of the monolith west of my campsite

Day - 50.
Hipko and two others arrived at my camp today. Communication is no longer a barrier. With strange words, exaggerated facial expressions, and hand gestures, we have now a common language. They brought a shoulder of deer meat. We sat before a fire and ate heartily enjoying each other's company. The closeness of the huge monolith still gives them caution. They do not venture beyond my campsite. I did find them more at ease, and they remained awhile. I beleive Hipko would join me in my explorations if it were not for the strong influence set by his society. When evening approached, however, and the large looming object gave off a soft moan they became fidgety, and they told me if they did not return to the villiage they would be missed. I was then clearly informed they were not afraid. And they added, a man who did not acknowledge the existence of foolishness is inviting many headaches. It was also at this time I learned the meaing of the name given to me by the villagers, "Odd Foolish One". They then departed into the darkness of the forest.

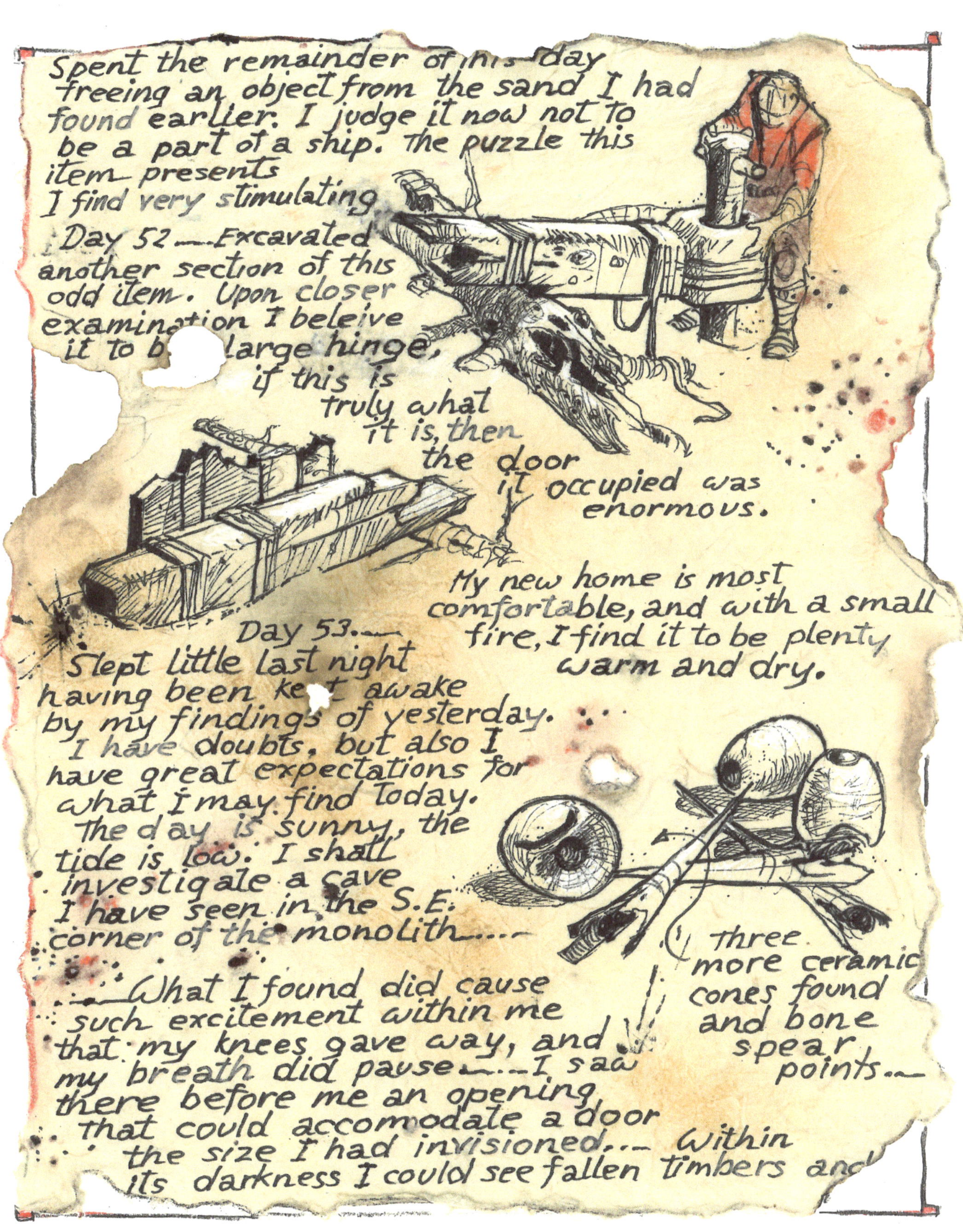

Spent the remainder of this day
freeing an object from the sand I had
found earlier. I judge it now not to
be a part of a ship. The puzzle this
item presents
I find very stimulating

Day 52 — Excavated
another section of this
odd item. Upon closer
examination I beleive
it to be a large hinge,
if this is
truly what
it is, then
the door
it occupied was
enormous.

My new home is most
comfortable, and with a small
fire, I find it to be plenty
warm and dry.

Day 53 —
Slept little last night
having been kept awake
by my findings of yesterday.
I have doubts, but also I
have great expectations for
what I may find Today.
The day is sunny, the
tide is low. I shall
investigate a cave
I have seen in the S.E.
corner of the monolith....

What I found did cause
such excitement within me
that my knees gave way, and
my breath did pause.... I saw
there before me an opening
that could accomodate a door
the size I had invisioned.... Within
its darkness I could see fallen timbers and

three
more ceramic
cones found
and bone
spear
points....

stone
work
much like
that of the pillars.
Some with markings
upon them.
Others with
bowl shaped
hollows that
I conclude to be the
sockets on which the
large hinge, I before
found, would fit. This I
now know to be more
than a natural structure,
for much is built by
man. Looking within this large gaping opening,
I could see shadows and silhouettes of
many things that did tempt me to enter. And
I saw steps....leading to some further
mysteries.

this evening I sit comfortably in
my shelter sketching the
abundance of evidence I have
collected today. It allows me to
beleive that this is an
accurate depiction of that
great door...... The
lateness of day forbade
my going within...but
go within I shall!
tomorrow when the
tide is low.
Watching the setting
sun the incoming
tide surrounding
this huge silhouette
with a natural moat,
I do understand
why this rocky
point was
chosen as
its location.
It affords a
po
that
one of
safty

Ceffsky's own words: "I found a structure of such grand proportions that I find description difficult. I realize why the natives fear this place. It fills me with apprehension and awe. The wind and waves coiling their way

through its cavities and crevices would explain those eerie sounds oft heard on dark, stormy nights—
haunting sounds again heard in their lodges, where they were duplicated in song and dance."

Many more pages in the professor's journals were devoted to this enormous chamber, which he called "Harbor Hall." Sadly, most of the pages dealing with its details were in such a state of decay, that only fragments of information remain. What did emerge, however, was the mood of excitement he felt after entering the structure and discovering the abundance of artifacts that lay within.

decide
are some kind of

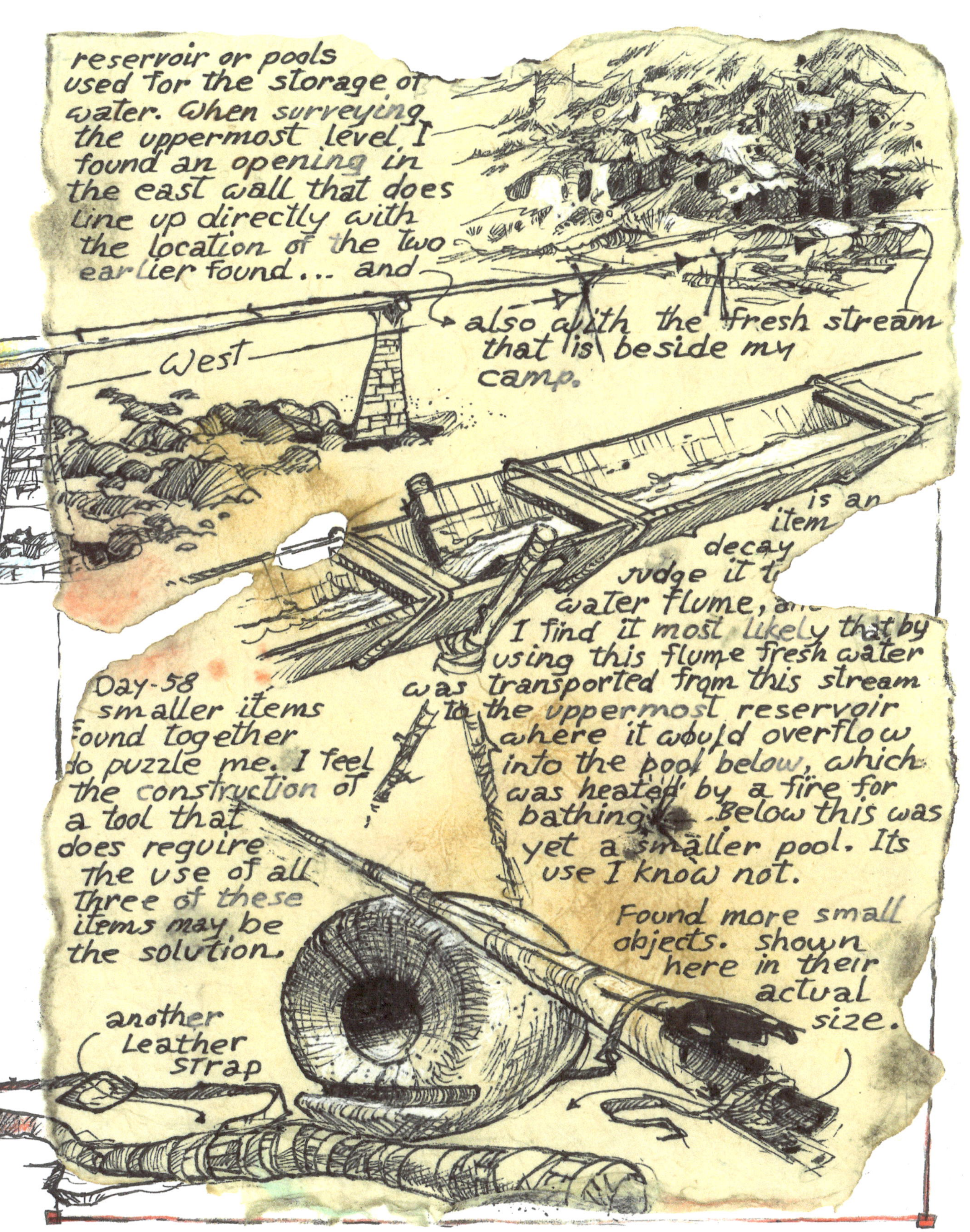

reservoir or pools used for the storage of water. When surveying the uppermost level, I found an opening in the east wall that does line up directly with the location of the two earlier found... and

West

also with the fresh stream that is beside my camp.

is an item decay judge it t water flume, and I find it most likely that by using this flume fresh water was transported from this stream to the uppermost reservoir where it would overflow into the pool below, which was heated by a fire for bathing. Below this was yet a smaller pool. Its use I know not.

Day-58 smaller items found together do puzzle me. I feel the construction of a tool that does require the use of all three of these items may be the solution.

Found more small objects. shown here in their actual size.

another Leather Strap

and with great care manage to take
the soggy mass of material and
flatten it out for identification. It
was, I discovered, to be a form of
footware. A few small tacks I find
still imbeded in the leather, which
surprised me greatly for it did
show these people had knowledge
to forge metal, which I believe
to be a kind
of copper.

the structure, were moved about. this
sketch is only speculation, but these
magnificient mammals are in abundance.
Large wheels with partial axle and yoke
were found, to which many lengths of
leather rope were attached.

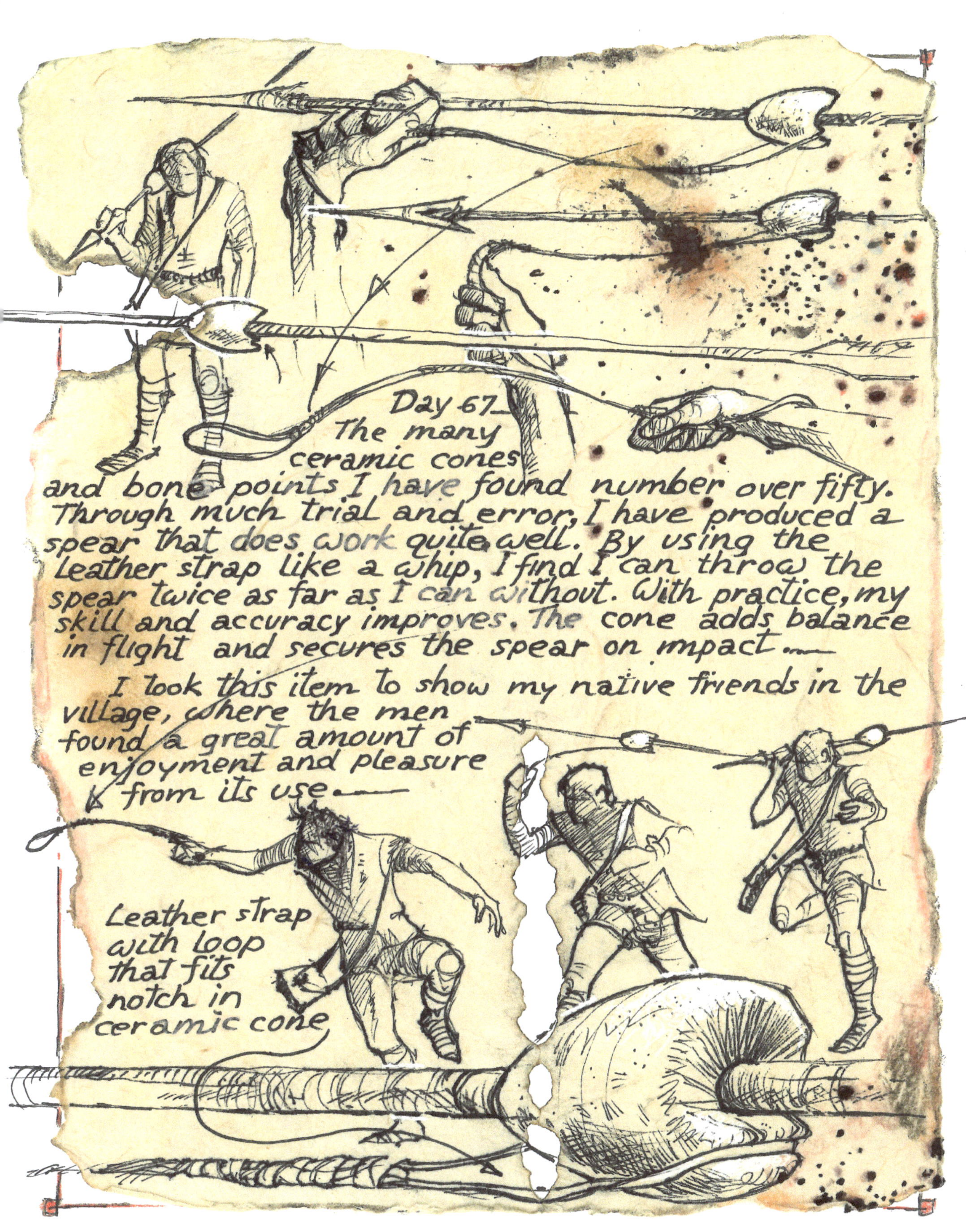

Day 67
The many
ceramic cones
and bone points I have found number over fifty.
Through much trial and error, I have produced a
spear that does work quite well. By using the
leather strap like a whip, I find I can throw the
spear twice as far as I can without. With practice, my
skill and accuracy improves. The cone adds balance
in flight and secures the spear on impact.

I took this item to show my native friends in the
village, where the men
found a great amount of
enjoyment and pleasure
from its use.

Leather strap
with loop
that fits
notch in
ceramic cone

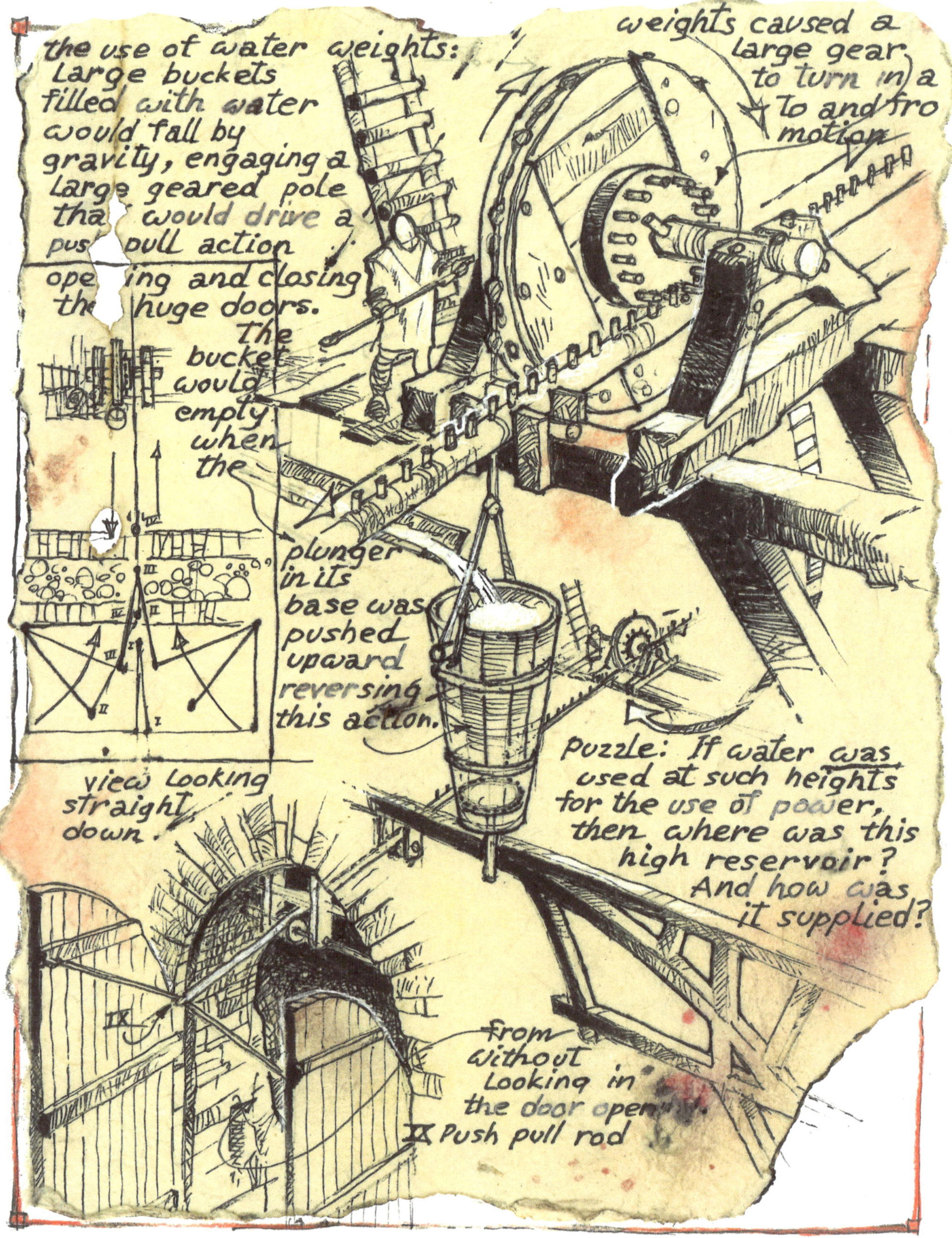

the use of water weights:
large buckets
filled with water
would fall by
gravity, engaging a
large geared pole
that would drive a
push pull action
opening and closing
the huge doors.
The
bucket
would
empty
when
the
plunger
in its
base was
pushed
upward
reversing
this action.
weights caused a
large gear
to turn in a
to and fro
motion
view looking
straight
down.
puzzle: If water was
used at such heights
for the use of power,
then where was this
high reservoir?
And how was
it supplied?
from
without
looking in
the door open
Push pull rod

I have found the high reservoir that supplies power to this edifice!
Day
I am
in a chamber
many measure
above the sea.
Here I find the
ruins of a
Windmill whose
mechanics are
used to raise
salt water to this level.
Also found was a portion of a belt, onto
which many cups are secured. Such a belt,
if it be continuous, would indeed keep this
reservoir well supplied! Power then could
this structure
does face S.W. the
direction of the
prevailing
winds.

So important was this section of the structures within the monolith, that the professor spent over a month studying its wonders. It was on this page of his journal that he intended to show the compilation of his research. Alas, only fragments were recovered. However, by using these remains, and other information relating to the area, we were able to reconstruct what he discovered in the chamber— a machine that harnessed the power of the waves.

a chamber of rooms so comfortable, I feel as if
I am in a castle. These rooms were occupied
by someone of importance, for they are grand
indeed. I shall now concentrate my search
to the south— to the area above the Harbor
Room ceiling.

I came upon an imposing stairway. The rise of each step was no more than four inches, and the tread took a full stride. Most certainly a caseway to a place of prominence. Reaching the top step, I moved forward cautiously for the light was fading. I found myself standing in a large cavernous chamber; the ceiling above disappeared into the darkness. The walls to my left and to my right also vanished into the shadows. The remaining light fell on the wall before me, where I saw an interesting alcove protecting a recessed door. I took a step forward to explore it when I kicked free a bit of rubble which fell into darkness and splashed into water far below.

I was suddenly aware that I was standing on the edge of a deep crevasse and that small bit of rubble had saved my life. The landing on which I stood was smoothly paved with flagstone. I studied the door across the chasm. It was framed by an arched alcove. Three steps dropped from the door to a small ledge. This ledge, it appeared, was the only object protruding from the wall. I felt certain I could jump the distance with a quick run, but once on the other side, I would be stranded, for there was little room to maneuver. I turned to search for a board or plank anything sturdy enough to bridge the void.

Having found one suitable for the task, I stood it on end. Guiding it carefully, I let it fall to that far ledge. My aim was correct, but I misjudged the consequence of so heavy a weight striking the ledge. When it hit the ledge it caused me to lose my grip when it hit. It then bounced, spun around, and proceeded to follow the peice of rubble down that deep hole; crashing to water below. Discouraged, but still determined, I returned with another plank more suitable, one less stout and more manageable. With this I was successful in making the bridge. Fearful of walking the plank I straddled it, and slowly inched my way across. When I reached the other side I found the small ledge just and barely wide enough to stand on. There was rubble and debris scattered all about, which caused caused me to stumble. I lost my balance, and fell accidentally dislodging the plank, and it too careened down the abyss. My only avenue to freedom was gone. I now realized my situation was serious. I foolishly became so intent upon accomplishing my objective, that I had ignored the amount of light remaining. The sun had set and night was rapidly approaching. I turned to what had to be my only means of escape, the door. I frantically searched for a handle, a latch, a lock, something! There had to be something, but I found nothing. As light dwindled I explored its perimeter. Every surface of the alcove, the door, the steps, and those portions of the wall I could reach, all this my eyes and fingers explored. I found nothing. Discouraged, I slumped into that dark alcove to ponder my predicament as the last light deserted me. I was stranded, perched on the ledge of nothingness. Darkness was so black, so deep, even my hand before my face was invisible. I thoug   I could have had just three fingers instead of five and it would not be discernable. If darkne   was   ld be discribed as heavy, this was indeed a we   ght too great to endure. I hugged my knees, pull   them close to my chest. I sat huddled   ere precariously, afraid to move. "Perhaps tomor   w when the light returns." I berated myself for my foolishness and slept little that night. When morning came, I could see my situation more clearly, but it had not improved. The door, its alcove, the three steps, and the small ledge were all that protruded from the wall. My path to freedom was beyond my reach and the width of the cravasse was wider than I had thought. I stepped to the edge and peered down. I could not see the bottom yet, but I could hear the sound of the surf. Perhaps that was my way out. I turned to look at the door and studied it and the wall about it. All was mortared smooth. I could see no way a person could scale the wall, not a hole, gap, or crack was within my reach. Once again I turned my attention to the door, frantically searching for a clue as to its secret. If there were a device to unlock it, the whereabouts of this mechanism eluded me. — If ever there was a door to be used only by those intended few, then this was it! — I found no hinges or door latch, no evidence of any kind that would allow me entrance. If this door was to open, it was   to be opened from within! There was visible on   e portion of the wall that gave me any hope, and that was high up

and to the north. Here mortar had decayed, and a
section of the wall had crumbled, but it was
out of my reach. as light slowly traveled
over this part of the wall it caused the
shadows to change. I caught a glimpse
of indentation — poss- ibly where I could
find a grip, and a bit further on
I saw another handhold, a just
above that the
collapsed section
of wall. If only
I dare to reach
for it. I sat on
the stairs look-
ing across that
void calculating my
options. "I must not
panic", I thought.
If I were to make
a move, it must
be now while it
was light and I
still had strength.
I must move,
before thirst
and hunger
fell upon me
Lack of sleep was
already unwanted
visitor. I tried to give
no thought of the dark abyss below me and to
dwell only on a means scape. the facts
were simple, I could ously not go back the
way I had come, and it was an absolute —

certainty no one was coming to my rescue. I decided to jump for that handhold. I mustered my strength and dove for that gap in the wall. I was successful and I swung to another. I found myself just below the crumble section. Hoisting my body into its cavity, I found the stones there loose and mortar decayed. I began to clear the rubble, The rough abrasive material making my fingers raw. — A draft of cool air fell against my cheek. I searched to find its origin and found the vent. It was blocked by a large stone. Bracing myself against it, I shoved. It moved, slowly at first; then loosened and fell away. Fresh, cool, damp air greeted me. I had broken through. I wiggled and pulled myself through the hole. Stones, mortar and I slid on to a small balcony. I was exhausted, but free! I stood and looked about. the view from here was breath taking It seemed to go on forever. From this height I could see the native village, and the smoke from the fires rose up and twisted towards the sky.

Day 82 - My major concerns were three: first, I still needed to find a way back to my camp; second, I felt a renewed desire to explore these new surroundings; and third, the need to relieve the pain I had inflicted upon my body. It was not my wish to repeat yesterday's mistakes. I immediately proceeded to search for the other side of that door. I quickly left the balcony, passed through a small chamber, and came upon a long hallway, The floor of which inclined gently upward to my right. Looking left I saw it stopped abruptly, being halted by a large round stone taller than myself, and wider than my open hand. the stone was crafted beautifully. From its very center, designs and pictographs appeared completely covering the whole of the stone's flat surface. Only then did I see the other markings covering every surface visable to me: the walls, the ceiling, even the floor. I was astounded. No other place in this structure had I witnessed any evidence of writing. I now realized I had found proof that the occupants of this castle possessed the knowledge of communicating thought beyond speech. this demanded further study, and I did start up that long, spiraling hallway, but good senses brought me up short, and I returned, with some regret, to the more important issue, that door.

By a judgment of measure, the large round stone was itself the door. My hands and eyes studied it carefully. Halfway up the stone on the south side, a stone peg was inserted through a hole and on into the wall, securing it in position. I wondered why this necessary since the stone itself was of such tremendous weight. Who could possibly move it? There were evenly spaced holes about the outer circumference. I saw evidence of pulleys and ropes, all in a state of decay and rot and of no use to me. this was obviously not my way out. Perhaps further up the hallway I would find a.... then I thought..

A trickle of water ran down the hall into a groove below the stone, and disappeared. Another received the stone in the ceiling. their incline was slight, would it be enough I put my shoulder to the stone and pushed Nothing! or was there movement? wishful thinking! yet I believed it moved a little. Quickly I fell to my knees, and began removing sand and rubble from beneath the great stone itself. Suddenly, I heard a small rumble, then a loud crack; it began to move, almost smashing my fingers. I sprang back, falling solidly on my rump, and I watched in amazement as the huge form glided with ease down the channel, and came to a halt with a resounding thud. to my suprize I was looking at the alcove in which I had slept the night before, and across that fearful abyss, I once more saw the path that would lead me to safety.

Day- 86

I slept little last night. I was beset by thoughts of the day's venture.
With the rope over my shoulder I entered the Harbor Room and
proceeded to climb through those passage   that have become
so well known to me. I have reached the roo
                    I loo   here I saw

                                        grasped it and proceeded to
                                    thread, and worked my way to
        I could see through to the opposite wall where there
      a small door through which I could see stairs and objects
beyond. In one corner there were remains of a hearth. A small
window allowed light and the afternoon sun to penetrate and with
a fire it would have been a place of comfort. the height size of
the door opening wa   é lintel no higher than my armpit
Was this, I wondere   mportant di   that
    indicated the measur   o occup   8.
Exiting this chambe   my greatest
discovery to this date I   ed   was as grand as the Harbor
Room. I shouted aloud   echo filled the hall. Would anyone
anywhere ever know of my discoveries? Many nights I spent
writing in my journals sitting by the fire, in the center of the Great
Hall with the glow dancing across the ceiling. I slept surrounded
by all its wonders, all its questions and all the ghosts and
memories it held.

Ceffsky's own words: "I had found a castle! I had seen many Great Halls, but none so fine as this. I was
so preoccupied with its mystery and wonder, the incoming tide forced me to spend another night within

the monolith. I built a fire of such proportions that its sparkling light was sent into every corner of the hall. I fear the glow caused much uneasiness among my native friends when seen from their village."

After my extensive studies of the Great Hall
I have returned to the village to join in a celebrated
occasion. The running of the salmon that return
from the sea to flood the little river. Men, women,
and children are caught up in the frenzy of
this abundant harvest. Even I cannot resist
participating in the event. I fell to the task
with such abandon, that I brought great
amusement to my native friends. I was
soon drenched from head to toe, trying to
catch the slippery creatures. The natives
used spears, nets, and at times their
hands to catch and toss their
prey upon the shore. Women and
children wielding clubs of wood
then gave the blow that
rendered them limp while
others prepared the meat to
ensure the provisions needed
for the months that lay
before them. I shall extend
my stay in the village and
organize my
journals.

Four journal pages were produced by Professor Ceffsky illustrating his attempt to clarify one particular topic. These pages were drawings and dealt with an important part of his study of the castle. They were a visual index to his work, and he made repeated reference to them.

Unfortunately, their state of decay was extreme, and the bits and pieces of these pages were too delicate to handle repeatedly, making it essential they be carefully inspected only by infrared camera and electro microscope. With these methods, enough data was compiled for Mr. Steidel to render an approximation of the professor's work. These appear on the following pages.

Due to the importance the professor placed on this work, I have included layouts with some of the fragmented pieces along with my own written interpretation and studied suppositions. The intent is to allow readers a more complete glimpse of the professor's findings.

The evolution of the edifice was the subject of greatest interest to the professor. His desire to research the skill with which the builders achieved their engineering feats, and the examples of craftsmanship within the castle, fascinated him. He wondered if and where the division between the manmade portions and the natural rock formation could be found. The builders' expertise was in evidence everywhere, and the amalgamation of the two became his primary focus. Eventually, the way the professor went about his research took a daring turn. He chose to explore the structure from the outside—not an easy task considering the conditions under which he was working.

So there is little I can do with the weather being much rainy, but I spend many days inside the protective walls of the edifice working on some drawings. A large fire gives warmth and light and I do find good comfort even though the days be dark and gloomy. I continue to explore the wonders of natural rock formation and the craftsmanship by which it was built upon. So skillfully was it done that I find the joining to be at time difficult to be identified. I now compile series of drawings to show the evolution of this structure through the rigors of time. I try to date or relate my findings to other societies I have encountered. It is my desire to give a view of this edifice in such a way as to allow me to show the location of my discoveries. I find a sense of peace here among the shadows of those who so long ago vacated this grand monolith. The task is difficult but I feel in these few parchments that I have achieved a successful system. The drawings I produce of the structure are viewed from the southeast. I am designating areas of interest to be labeled "a" "b" "c" and so on if my discoveries go beyond these letters, which appears it well may do, the label "a1" "b1" "c1" will be used. By this method of indexing I shall associate discoveries with drawings. I chose the southeast view looking seaward at low tides. Even when stranded by the surrounding sea I have a good amount of comfort. there are many rooms that are now farmiliar to me and my nights are spent before a fire listening to the wind make mysterious sounds as it forces its way through the many convoluted passages I have yet to find.

It is because of these many passages blocked by cave ins and cavernous voids that are too difficult to cross that I find it a dangerous task, but a necessary one. the leather and vine rope made by my native friends is wearing well and it permits me to enter sections unavailable to me before.

I miss my visits to the village, and a chance to practice their language. It has recently become unpleasant. Hipko and his friends in the village have avoided me. Some speak to me not at all. Seeing me climbing about this feared monolith has caused an irritation in our relationship. What I do must seem to them truly foolish. An act of total abandonment or perhaps to them it is a taboo or an insult. I do not know. It concerns me in moments of melancholy, but my work is too important. I have tried to explain to them my need to explore, but they do not understand. They will cover their ears and shake their heads. Not all connection has been severed, however, for often I return to my hut in the trees only to find a side of meat or some little offering.

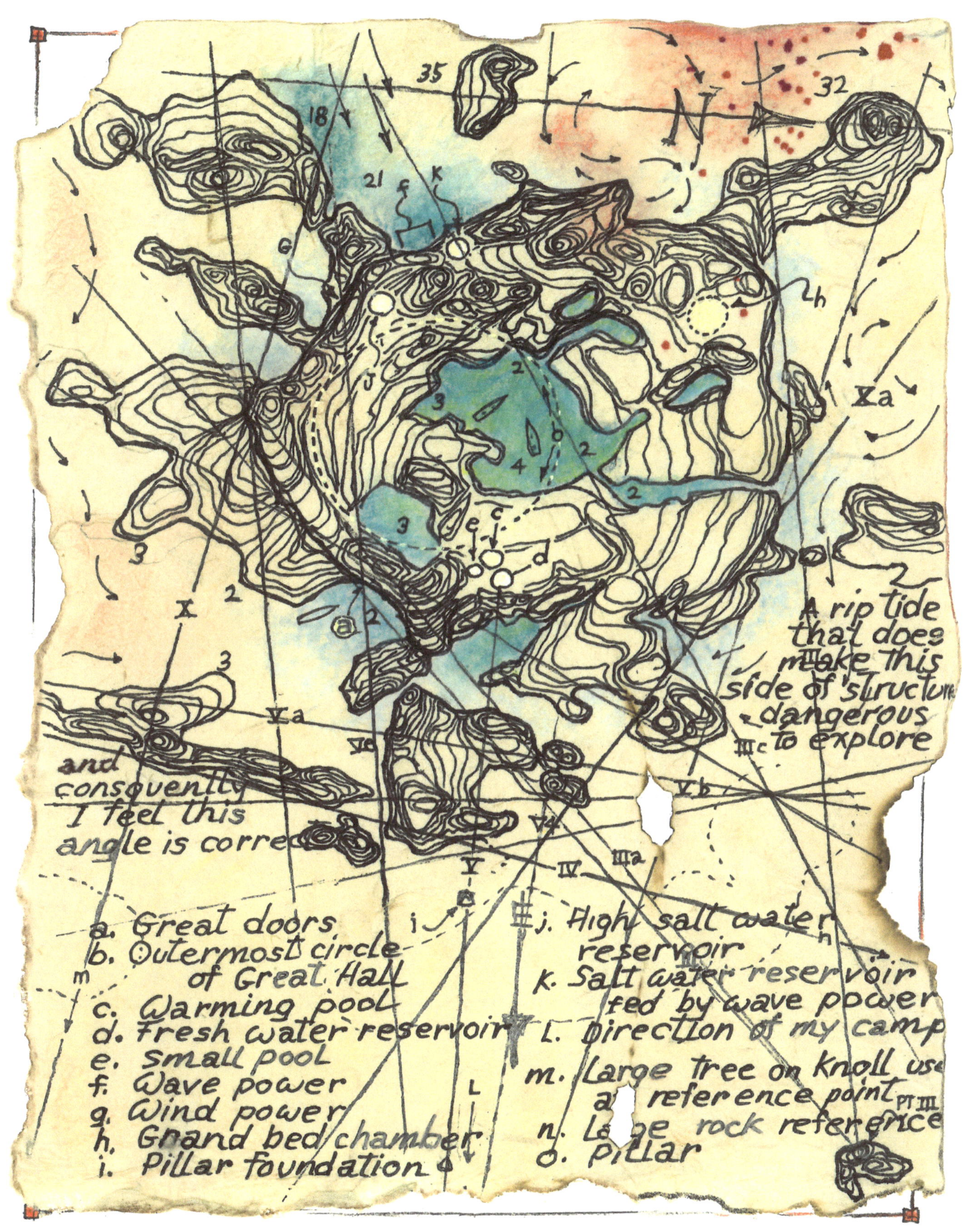

35
32
N
18
21
Xa
h
X
Va
Vc
Vb
IIIc
IIIa
IV
V
Y
i
L
m
A rip tide that does make this side of structure dangerous to explore
and consequently I feel this angle is correct
a. Great doors
b. Outermost circle of Great Hall
c. Warming pool
d. Fresh water reservoir
e. Small pool
f. Wave power
g. Wind power
h. Grand bed chamber
i. Pillar foundation
j. High salt water reservoir
k. Salt water reservoir fed by wave power
l. Direction of my camp
m. Large tree on knoll used a reference point
n. Large rock reference
o. Pillar
PT III

and it is my desire to show the original rock foundation the large castle was built on, and I wonder what will time leave for the future. the weather is gloomy, and I have spent many rainy days and nights; I find now there are many, searching out the secrets of this grand Castle. I have done the best I could to try to separate what was built and what was built on, what was natural, and what was made by man. However, it is the weaving together of these two that make the Castle so unique. Although have not seen it in its finished form, what I have

The exact age of Professor Eff Ceffsky's journals is unknown. With research, however, it was possible to estimate their age. They were written approximately two hundred years before the Lewis and Clark Expedition arrived at the same location on the coast of Oregon. They found direct descendants of the villagers who ate and drank with the professor. The parchment journal pages found were filled with sketches and observations by the professor about the native people, the local coastal area, and the castle. With this last notation of the professor's, I close my initial study of Castle Haystack. Some of the pages found were caked with mud and in need of much love and care and are still in the process of being restored. Perhaps at some future date, if more of the journal parchments are made available, further study may be warranted. But, for now, I shall call my efforts complete. As an epilogue to this study, on several pages to follow, I've included notatations discovered in the captain's log from the ship that rescued the professor.

Captain's Log—

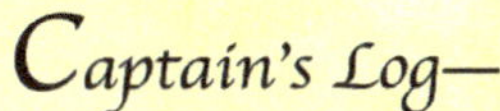

The well spoken but oddly dressed fellow we rescued two days ago, long marooned on the isolated, rugged coastline, has become upset. Frantic in fact. Items of great importance to him are missing from his chest, the only object brought aboard with him. He says it is something about research he has done about a castle and writings on parchments made from deerskins.

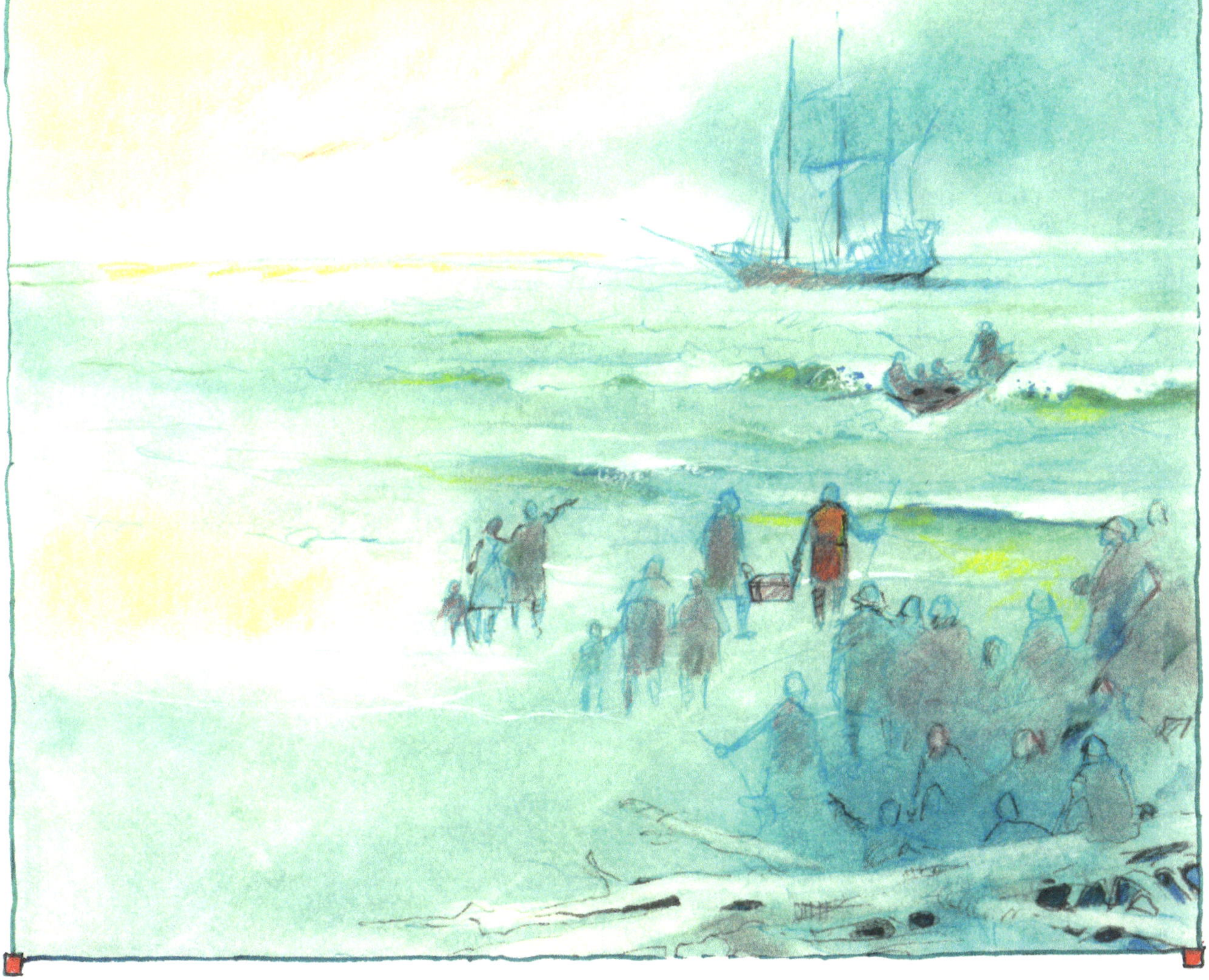

$\mathcal{A}$ search of the ship was conducted in the hope of calming him. Nothing was found. His sanity was in question until his outburst subsided. He finally calmed and gave up his search, convinced that his native friends, out of fear, had not allowed his journals to leave their shore.

Captain's log—

Three weeks out from our last anchorage, I find our passenger an odd man indeed, but well educated and good company, except when melancholy falls upon him, due most assuredly to the loss of his journals.

On October 5, 1999, a well known, longtime resident of Cannon Beach, and an experienced beachcomber, came upon three objects uncovered by a recent storm. They were cones, exactly like those described in the journals of Professor Eff Ceffsky. He kept one cone, he gave the second one to our illustrator, Mr. William W. Steidel, and the third one was sent to an institute in Washington, D. C. for further study.

On the southeast side of Haystack Rock, near the water's edge, can be found a cave—the last remaining evidence of Castle Haystack's large doors. With care, it is possible to line up your subject for a photo with the cave and the castle behind, and then place it in the space below.

If you find a small, oval, ceramic object similar to the ones shown in this book, please take it to Steidel's Art gallery in Cannon Beach for verification.

ACKNOWLEDGEMENT

I wish to thank the person who gave me access to Professor Eff Ceffsky's journal pages. The opportunity to read and examine the parchments was critical to this study. Restoration is on-going and far from complete. For the trust and responsibility that was allowed me, I shall be forever grateful.

WILLIAM W. STEIDEL

In the window of a small, rustic gallery on the corner of First and Hemlock Street in the village of Cannon Beach, Oregon, the artist, William Steidel can often be found. He sits behind a simple but ingenious swing-out easel, surrounded by a hodgepodge of artistic tools and paraphernalia. Here, Bill produces his particular brand of magic. He creates works of art, spins yarns, makes music, watches the passing parade of people, and delights in the view of the lush green mountains that lie in the distance.

The passions of artistic philosophy emerged very early in Bill's life on a small farm in Newburgh, New York. His work has progressed through the years from his time spent as a student at Columbia University, Pratt Institute, Northern Arizona University, and the University of Oregon, to his ensuing life experiences. Bill's journey inspired him to open his first independent gallery and studio in Cannon Beach in the 1950s. Inside the present-day gallery is a touch of whimsy and wonder, and if you are fortunate, you are apt to find a bit of yourself present on the gallery's walls.

"Art, I find, is an emotional food. It gives us nourishment. We feed on its many forms, and if at times it jars too roughly, tickles too uncomfortably, or soothes too frequently, it would, if not available, be sorely missed. If we were unfortunate enough to lose it, we would once more create it so we could debate why it is so very necessary."